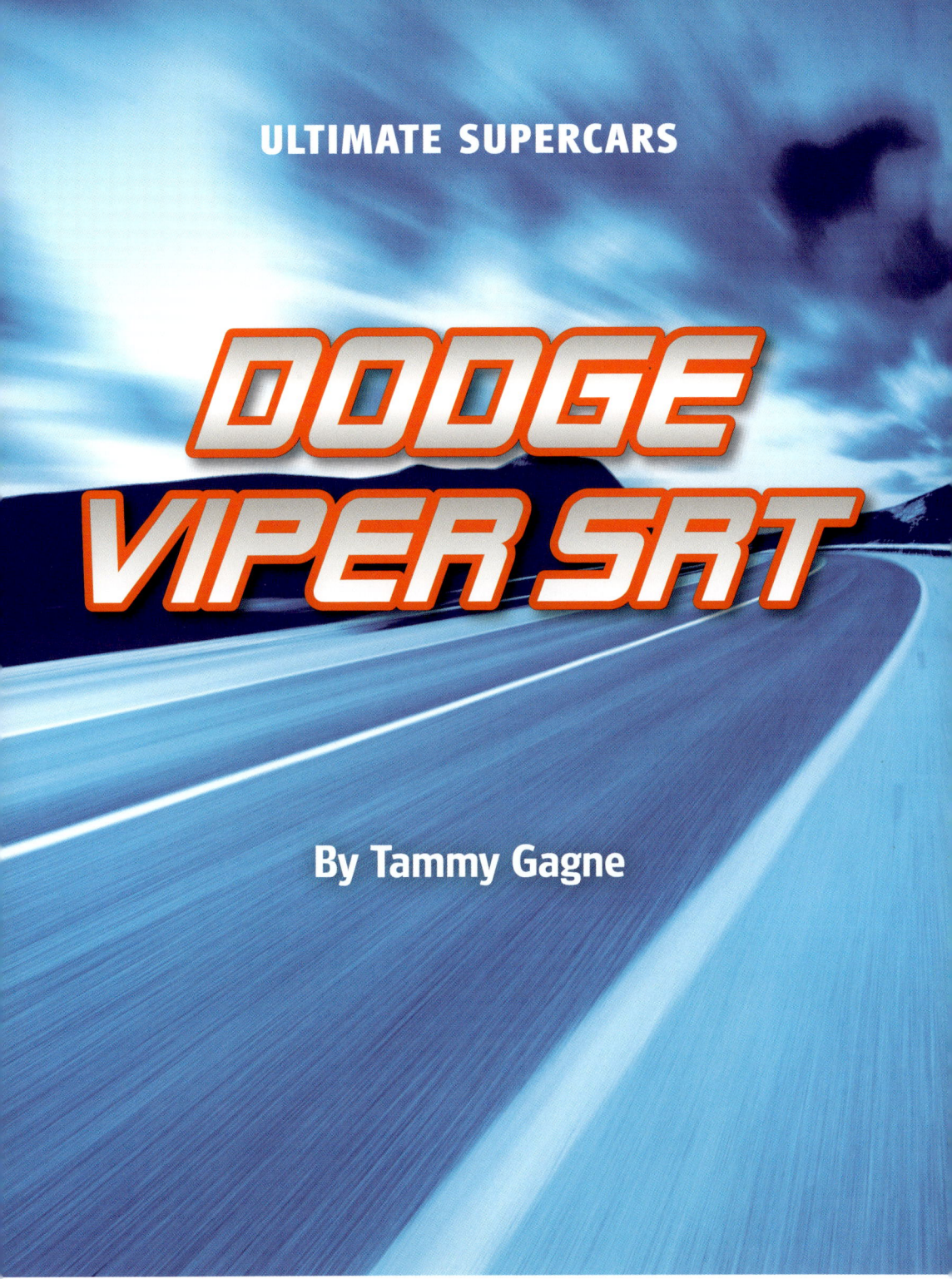

ULTIMATE SUPERCARS

DODGE VIPER SRT

By Tammy Gagne

Kaleidoscope
Minneapolis, MN

The Quest for Discovery Never Ends

This edition is co-published by agreement between Kaleidoscope and World Book, Inc.

Kaleidoscope Publishing, Inc.
6012 Blue Circle Drive
Minnetonka, MN 55343 U.S.A.

World Book, Inc.
180 North LaSalle St., Suite 900
Chicago IL 60601 U.S.A.

All rights reserved. No part of this book may be reproduced in any form without written permission from the publishers.

Kaleidoscope ISBNs
978-1-64519-027-1 (library bound)
978-1-64494-234-5 (paperback)
978-1-64519-127-8 (ebook)

World Book ISBN
978-0-7166-4328-9 (library bound)

Library of Congress Control Number
2019940225

Text copyright ©2020 by Kaleidoscope Publishing, Inc. All-Star Sports, Bigfoot Books, and associated logos are trademarks and/or registered trademarks of Kaleidoscope Publishing, Inc.

Printed in the United States of America.

FIND ME IF YOU CAN!

Bigfoot lurks within one of the images in this book. It's up to you to find him!

TABLE OF CONTENTS

Chapter 1: 3, 2, 1—Go! 4

Chapter 2: The Birth of the Viper 10

Chapter 3: One Fast Car 16

Chapter 4: Still a Treasure 22

Beyond the Book 28

Research Ninja 29

Further Resources 30

Glossary 31

Index 32

Photo Credits 32

About the Author 32

CHAPTER 1

3, 2, 1—GO!

The sun shone on the track. A crowd waited in the stands. A fun event was about to begin. Ethan was excited. He was also nervous. He was racing his 2003 Dodge Viper SRT. He had owned it for years. But he had never raced it before. Now he sat behind its wheel. He wore a racing helmet. People were cheering for him.

Another supercar was beside him. The other driver revved her engine. Ethan looked at her. He wondered if she was nervous. He knew his car was fast. But was it fast enough? Everyone would find out soon.

The 2003 Dodge Viper SRT-10 was the second generation of the Dodge Viper.

Ethan was driving for charity. The prize was $1,000. He wanted to win. The flags dropped. Ethan sped ahead of the other car. The Viper did not let him down.

He watched the **speedometer**. It reached 60 miles per hour (97 km). Had he done it in 3.9 seconds? That's what the magazines said the Viper could do. Ethan went faster.

The SRT-10 was made from 2003 to 2010.

He'd never driven this fast. He usually had a speed limit. This felt amazing.

He reached the first curve. The other driver was gaining on him. But he pulled ahead. Her car was fast. It just wasn't as fast as the Viper.

PARTS OF A
2008 DODGE VIPER SRT

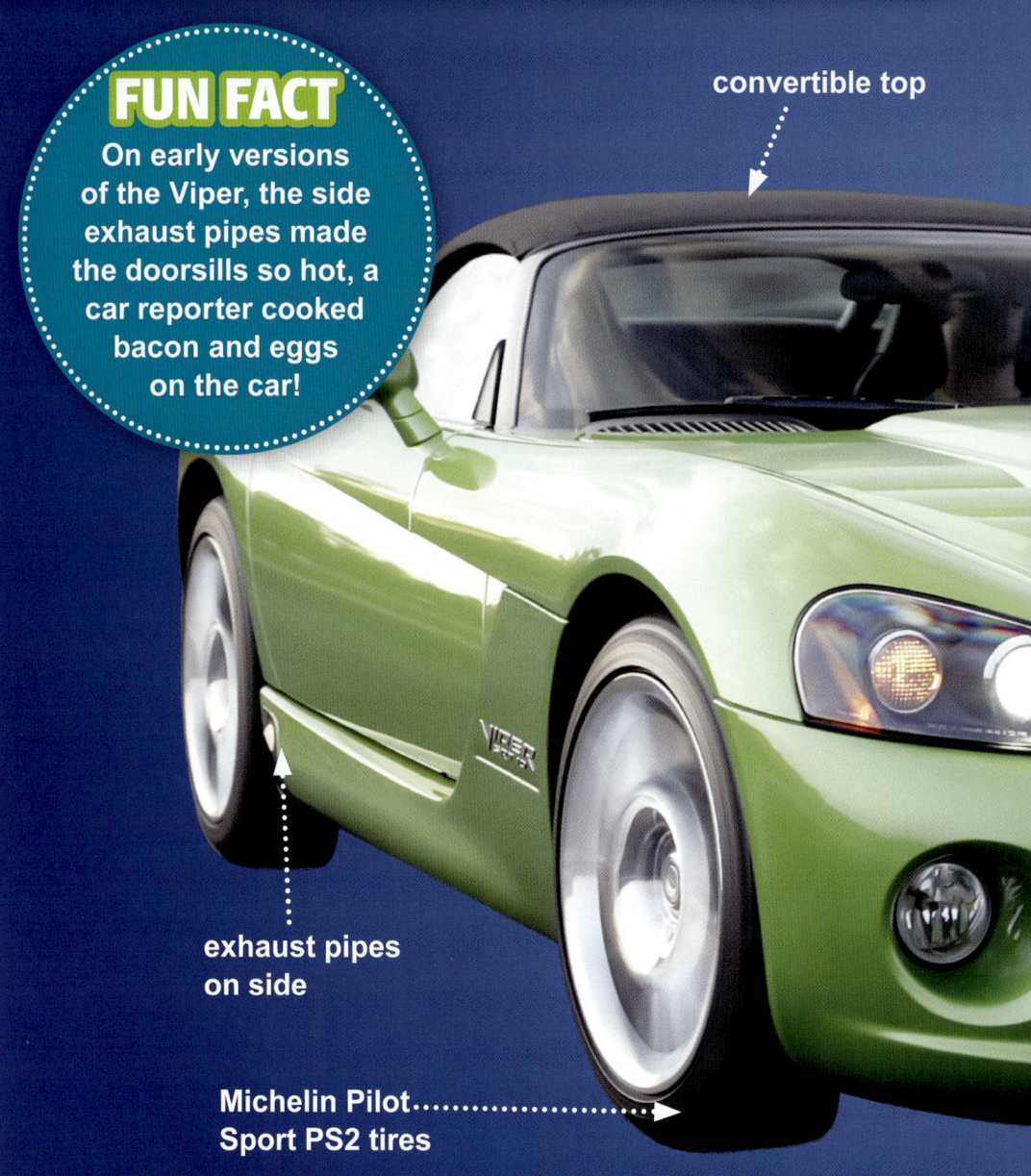

FUN FACT
On early versions of the Viper, the side exhaust pipes made the doorsills so hot, a car reporter cooked bacon and eggs on the car!

convertible top

exhaust pipes on side

Michelin Pilot Sport PS2 tires

The Viper SRT had 500 **horsepower**. Ethan could feel this power. He drove out of the second curve. The gap between the drivers widened. He could see the checkered flag. He was really going to do it. He would win the race! It was thanks to his Dodge Viper SRT.

hood vents

"Fangs" Viper logo

CHAPTER 2

THE BIRTH OF THE VIPER

The year is 1988. Bob Lutz is the president of Chrysler Motors. This company owns Dodge. But Lutz doesn't drive a Chrysler. He drives a Ford Cobra instead. Chrysler doesn't make a supercar. Lutz decides to change this.

He chooses a team of car designers. He gives them a special task. He asks them to create a supercar. It must be better than the Cobra. The new car is a secret project. Few people at Chrysler know what's coming.

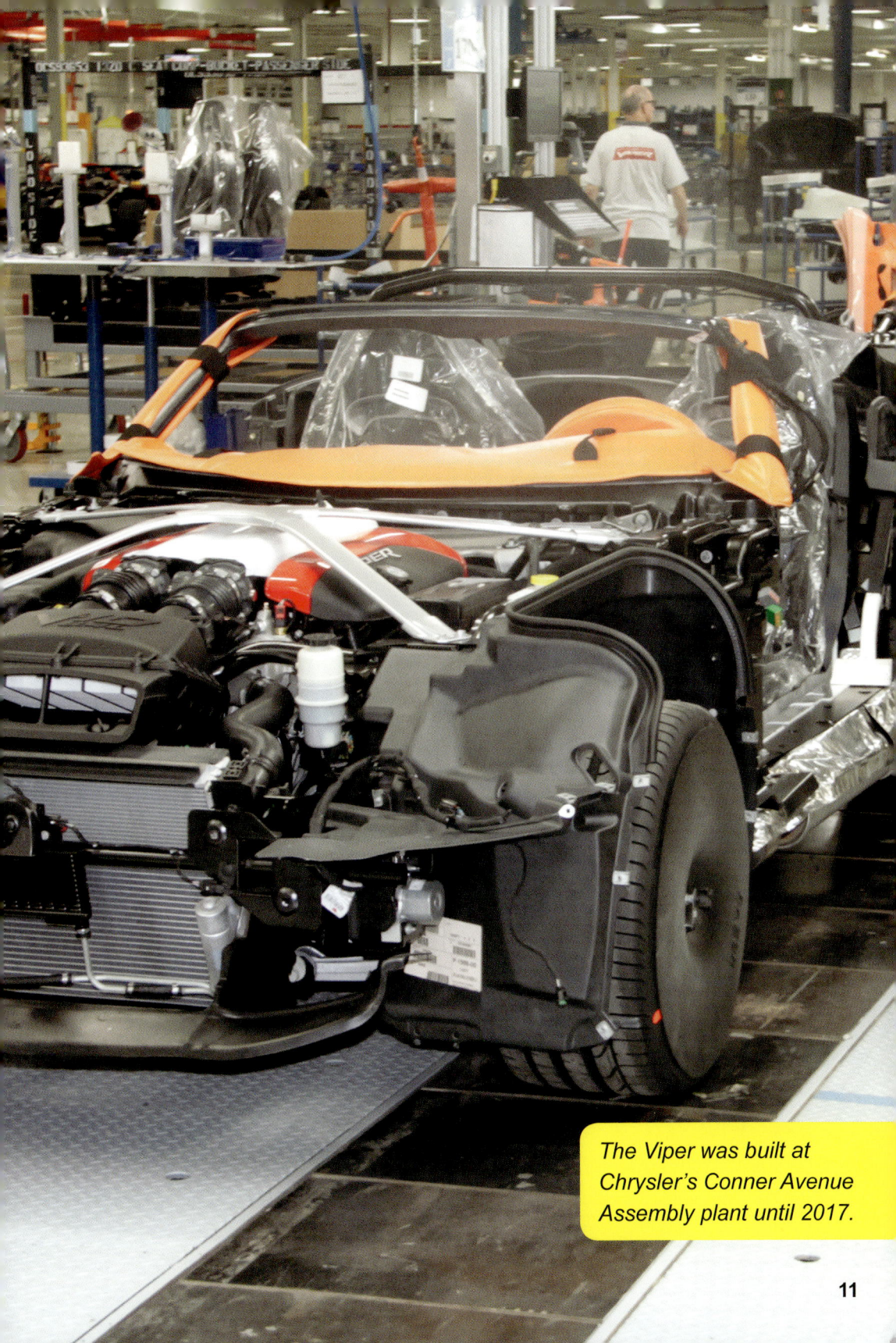

The Viper was built at Chrysler's Conner Avenue Assembly plant until 2017.

Where the Dodge Viper Was Made

1 **Detroit, Michigan:** Conner Avenue Assembly Plant, where the Dodge Viper was built

2 **Auburn Hills, Michigan:** Dodge headquarters

The car they designed became the Dodge Viper. It had a **sleek** look. And it was as fast as it looked. It had a **V10** engine. The same engine was used by Lamborghini. This Italian company is known for making fast sports cars.

HOW THE VIPER CHANGED

The first Dodge Viper was a **convertible**. Chrysler redesigned the Viper in 1996. It added a hard top. The company kept improving the supercar. The 1992 Viper had 400 horsepower. The SRT Viper had 640 horsepower by 2017.

FUN FACT

Each generation of the Viper got a new logo: "Sneaky Pete" (1992–2002), "Fangs" (2003–2010), and "Stryker" (2013–2017).

Stryker

Lutz introduced his new supercar to the world. Chrysler showed off the **prototype** in Detroit, Michigan. It was at the North American International Auto Show. This was in 1989. Lutz's team hoped people would like the Viper concept. They put a lot of work into its design. But they had no idea what would come. People loved it! Chrysler received orders before the car show ended. But it wasn't for sale yet.

More people saw the supercar in 1991. It was at the Indianapolis 500 race. The Viper was the **pace car**. It went on sale to the public later that year. It was a 1992 model. The rest is history.

The Viper prototype was revealed in 1989.

The 1992 Viper had no roof, windows, or outside door handles. There was also no air conditioning!

FUN FACT

A TV show called *Viper* ran from 1994–1999. It was about a high-tech Viper that was used to solve crimes.

CHAPTER 3

ONE FAST CAR

Jasmine looked around the parking lot. Her meeting would start soon. The SRT Viper's owner was not there yet. She hoped the car was everything he described. She already knew lots about the 2013 model. She had wanted one for years. Now she finally had the money to buy it.

Jasmine loved the car's color. It was called Adrenaline Red. It looked great with the black racing stripes.

The stripes made it look like a race car. The Viper drove like one, too. Its top speed was 206 miles per hour (332 km/h).

Jasmine had always loved supercars. She read about them. The 2013 Viper improved on previous models. It had 640 horsepower. That was 40 more than the 2010 model. It was also lighter. That meant it could go faster.

The SRT Viper was completely redesigned for 2013.

THE SRT VIPER
IN DETAIL

Height: 4.1 feet (1.2 m)

Width: 6.4 feet (2 m)

- Length: 14.6 feet (4.5 m)
- Weight: 3,300 pounds (1,497 kg)
- Top Speed: 206 miles per hour (332 km/h)
- Time from 0–60 miles per hour (0–97 km/h): 3.5 seconds

COST: $99,390

She saw her dream car pull into the lot. Her heart raced. The owner stepped out. He introduced himself. "Would you like to drive it?" he asked. Was he kidding? She hadn't thought of anything else today!

Jasmine sat behind the wheel. She adjusted the pedals. She could move them toward her. There was a navigation system. There was also a backup camera. These features surprised her. Vipers were usually known for being fast. They weren't known for being fancy. The 2013 model changed that.

The SRT Viper had a touch screen media center.

Now it was time to drive. Jasmine pulled out of the lot. She headed for the highway. She reached 60 miles per hour (97 km/h). It took 3.5 seconds. The ride was quieter than she expected. But she could still hear the engine. It made her feel powerful. She couldn't go top speed on the highway. But she could still feel the engine's power. The Viper was as fun to drive as it was to look at. It was all she had hoped it would be. Now she just had to get a good deal.

FUN FACT
The SRT Viper made a list of Top 10 Most American Cars in 2014 for being 75 percent American-made.

The SRT Viper had more power and speed than the original 1992 Viper.

WHAT DOES SRT MEAN?

The Dodge Viper was made from 1992–2017. "SRT" was part of its name from 2003–2017. SRT stands for "street and racing technology." The SRT group designed and built the first Viper. SRT works on sporty models of other Dodge vehicles. They include the Challenger, Charger, and Durango.

CHAPTER 4

STILL A TREASURE

Brian and Zane turned on their favorite podcast. It was all about cars. They listened every Thursday afternoon. The boys were huge Viper fans. They enjoyed hearing all the latest news. But bad news came in 2015. The hosts confirmed the rumors. Chrysler decided to stop making the Viper. Production would end in 2017.

Dodge stopped producing the Viper in 2017 after low sales.

The announcement wasn't surprising. The Viper hadn't sold well recently. But it was hard to hear. Could their favorite supercar really go away? They hated to see it happen.

Brian paused the podcast. "I can't believe it," he said.

"I was hoping they might just skip a couple years. You know, like in 2011," Zane said.

"Exactly," Brian said. Chrysler filed for **bankruptcy** in 2009. It stopped making the Dodge Viper SRT in 2010. It brought back a new model in 2013. This was the SRT Viper. But it was happening again. Poor sales were hurting the Viper. It would go out of production.

THE LAST TWO VIPERS MADE

The last Viper rolled off the assembly line. It was made in 2017. It was red. It had chrome wheels. Chrysler kept it for its history collection. The last Viper sold to a customer was yellow. It had black racing stripes. A couple in Texas bought it.

FUN FACT
Dodge made five special-edition Vipers to mark the end of Viper production in 2017.

The 2017 Viper Snakeskin Edition was one of the Viper special editions. The racing stripes had a snakeskin pattern.

Fans of the Viper were sad to see it go. Many hold out hope that it may come back.

Rumors began to spread. People said the supercar might come back. They hinted at a 2021 model. Fans hoped it was true. But Chrysler put these rumors to rest in 2019. It said there were no plans to bring the car back. The Viper was one of the best sports cars ever sold. But it just wasn't selling as well as other supercars.

The Viper remains popular with car collectors. Older models may become more valuable. This is because it's no longer being made. People who love this supercar still hold out hope. Maybe it will return someday.

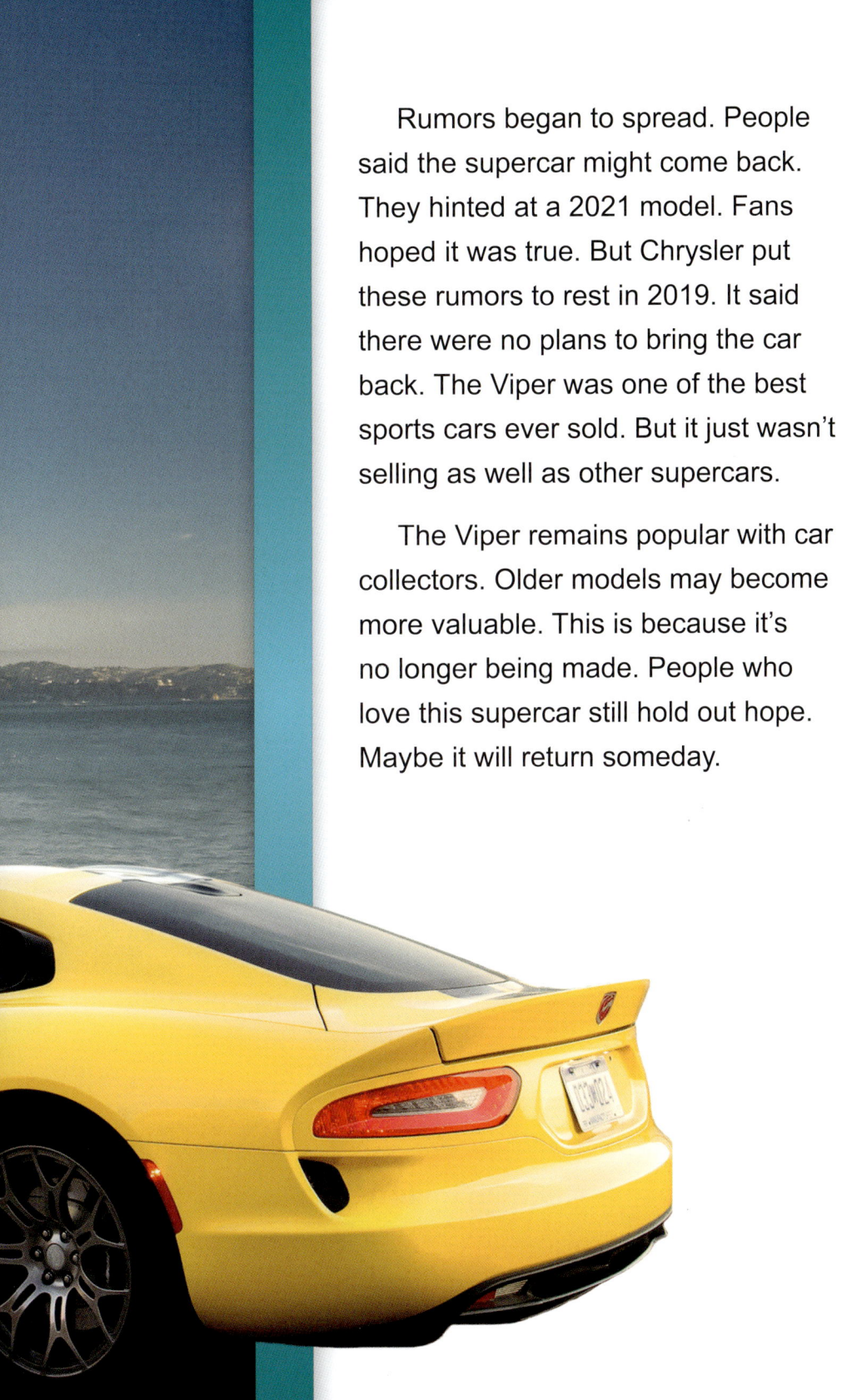

BEYOND THE BOOK

After reading the book, it's time to think about what you learned. Try the following exercises to jumpstart your ideas.

THINK

DIFFERENT SOURCES. Think about what types of sources you could find on the Dodge Viper SRT. What could you find in an encyclopedia? What could you learn at a car dealership? What about an interview with a mechanic? How could each of the sources be useful in its own way?

CREATE

PRIMARY SOURCES. A primary source is an original document, photograph, or interview. Make a list of different primary sources you might be able to find about the Dodge Viper SRT. What new information might you learn from these sources?

SHARE

WHAT'S YOUR OPINION? This book states that the Dodge Viper is one of the best sports cars ever sold. Do you agree or disagree with this position? Use evidence from the text to support your answer. Share your position and evidence with a friend. Does your friend agree with you?

GROW

REAL-LIFE RESEARCH. What places could you visit to learn more about the Dodge Viper SRT? What other things could you learn while you were there?

RESEARCH NINJA

Visit *www.ninjaresearcher.com/0271* to learn how to take your research skills and book report writing to the next level!

RESEARCH

DIGITAL LITERACY TOOLS

SEARCH LIKE A PRO
Learn about how to use search engines to find useful websites.

FACT OR FAKE?
Discover how you can tell a trusted website from an untrustworthy resource.

TEXT DETECTIVE
Explore how to zero in on the information you need most.

SHOW YOUR WORK
Research responsibly—learn how to cite sources.

WRITE

GET TO THE POINT
Learn how to express your main ideas.

PLAN OF ATTACK
Learn prewriting exercises and create an outline.

DOWNLOADABLE REPORT FORMS

FURTHER RESOURCES

BOOKS

Cruz, Calvin. *Dodge Viper SRT*. Bellwether Media, 2016.

Mason, Paul. *American Supercars: Dodge, Chevrolet, Ford*. PowerKids Press, 2019.

Power, Bob. *Dodge Vipers*. Gareth Stevens, 2012.

WEBSITES

Factsurfer.com gives you a safe, fun way to find more information.

1. Go to www.factsurfer.com.
2. Enter "Dodge Viper SRT" into the search box and click 🔍.
3. Select your book cover to see a list of related websites.

GLOSSARY

bankruptcy: Bankruptcy is a legal process a person or company declares when it is unable to pay its debts. The company filed for bankruptcy after a poor year of sales.

convertible: A convertible is a car with a removable top. The driver put the convertible's top down on the sunny day.

horsepower: Horsepower is the power it takes to lift 550 pounds one foot in one second. The first Dodge Viper had 400 horsepower.

pace car: A pace car leads the cars in a race through a lap, but it doesn't participate in the race. The Dodge Viper was the pace car at the 1991 Indianapolis 500.

prototype: A prototype is a first model from which future models are designed. The prototype of the Dodge Viper was a big hit at the car show.

sleek: Something that is sleek is smooth and stylish. The Dodge Viper looked sleek.

speedometer: A speedometer is a display that tells how fast a vehicle is going. The driver saw on the speedometer that he was going too fast.

V10: A V10 engine has ten cylinders in the shape of a *V*. The Dodge Viper used a V10 engine from Lamborghini.

INDEX

bankruptcy, 24

car show, 14
Chrysler, 10, 13, 14, 22–27
Cobra, 10
convertible, 8–9, 13
cost, 18

dashboard, 6, 19

engine, 5, 13, 20
exhaust pipes, 8–9

horsepower, 9, 13, 17

Indianapolis 500, 14

Lamborghini, 13
logo, 8–9, 13
Lutz, Bob, 10, 14

size, 18
special editions, 24, 25
SRT (group), 21
steering, 7–9

top speed, 17, 18

Viper (TV show), 15

PHOTO CREDITS

The images in this book are reproduced through the courtesy of: FCA Media, front cover (car), pp. 3, 4, 6–7, 8–9, 10–11, 13, 14–15, 15, 16–17, 18 (car), 19, 20–21, 22–23, 24–25, 26, 26–27, 30; Watch The World/Shutterstock Images, front cover (road); Natursports/Shutterstock Images, pp. 4–5; Red Line Editorial, pp. 12, 18 (chart).

ABOUT THE AUTHOR

Tammy Gagne has written dozens of books for both adults and children. Her recent titles include *Ford Mustang Shelby GT350* in the Ultimate Supercars series and *Quarterbacks* in the NFL's Greatest Players series. She lives in northern New England with her husband, son, and a menagerie of pets.